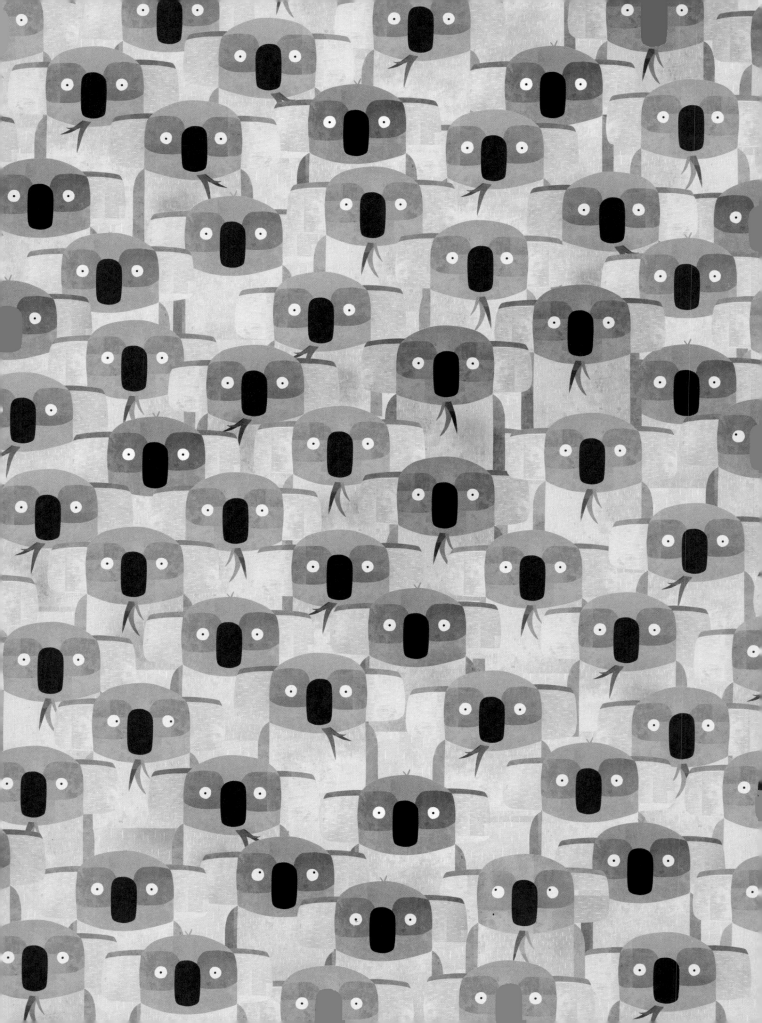

Koalas eat gum leaves.

LAURA + PHILIP BUNTING

An Omnibus Book from Scholastic Australia

This is a koala.

Koalas eat gum leaves.
Nothing but gum leaves.
All day. Every day.
So many gum leaves.

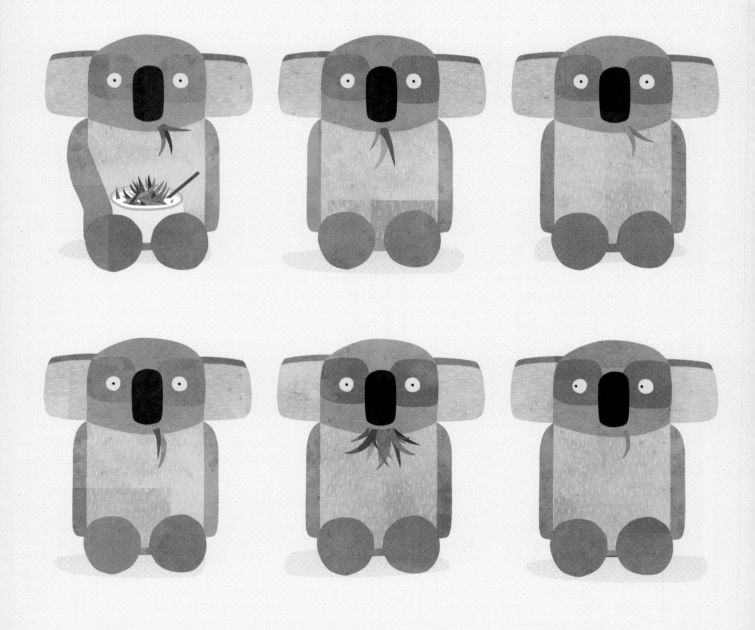

Gum leaves for breakfast.
Gum leaves for lunch.
Gum leaves for dinner.
With no exceptions...

Not even on their birthday.

Most koalas don't
seem to mind.

But this one
does.

This koala has had enough.
He won't eat another leaf.
Not another gumdrop.

He's on the lookout for
some tastier tucker.

No.

No!

Woah.

Hello!

Whoosh!

*By gum, that's good!

He runs.

He jumps.

He dances.

He cartwheels.

He goes back
for more.

Now this koala eats ice-cream.
Nothing but ice-cream.
All day. Every day.
So many ice-creams.

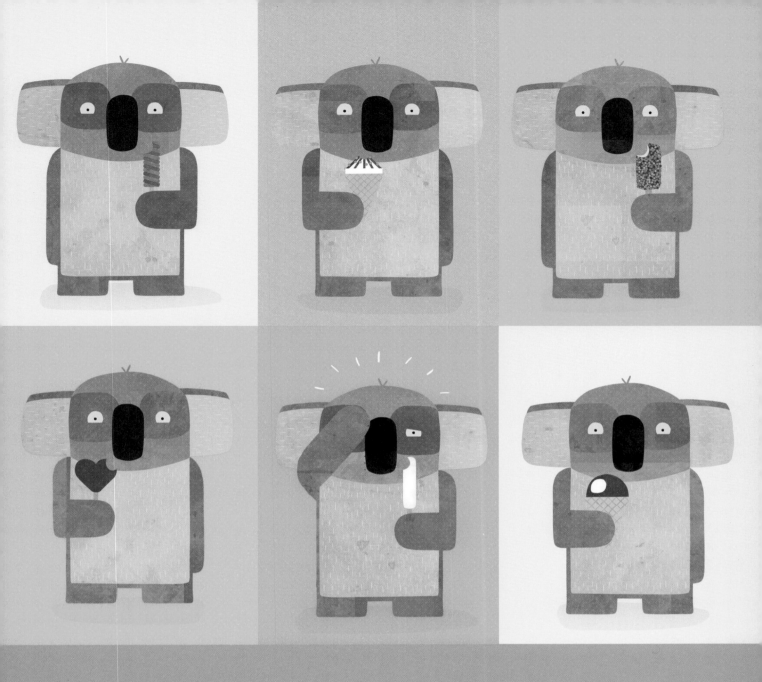

Ice-cream for breakfast.
Ice-cream for lunch.
Ice-cream for dinner.
With no exceptions...

Until one day, he'd had enough.
He couldn't eat another cone.
Not one more scoop.

It was time to go home.

#@$%!*

*By gum, this is hard work.

Koalas don't eat ice-cream.

Koalas eat gum leaves.

Even this one.

Most of the time.

FOR LEO,
WITH LOVE XX

Despite their monotonous diet, koalas are very fussy eaters.
There are around 700 varieties of gum leaf to choose from in
Australia, but koalas usually stick to just a few select species.

Omnibus Books
an imprint of Scholastic Australia Pty Ltd (ABN 11 000 614 577)
PO Box 579 Gosford NSW 2250
www.scholastic.com.au

Part of the Scholastic Group
Sydney • Auckland • New York • Toronto • London • Mexico City
• New Delhi • Hong Kong • Buenos Aires • Puerto Rico

Published by Scholastic Australia in 2017.
Text copyright © Laura Bunting, 2017.
Illustrations copyright © Philip Bunting, 2017.

National Library of Australia Cataloguing-in-Publication entry
Creator: Bunting, Laura, author.
Title: Koalas eat gum leaves / Laura Bunting ; Philip Bunting, illustrator.
ISBN: 978-1-74299-183-2 (hardback)
978-1-74299-184-9 (paperback)
Target Audience: For preschool age.
Subjects: Koala—Juvenile fiction
Koala—Feeding and feeds—Juvenile fiction
Ice cream, ices, etc.—Juvenile fiction.
Other Creators/Contributors: Bunting, Philip, illustrator.

Typeset in Apercu.

Printed in China by RR Donnelley.
Scholastic Australia's policy, in association with RR Donnelley, is to use papers that
are renewable and made efficiently from wood grown in responsibly managed forests,
so as to minimise its environmental footprint.

10 9 8 7 6 5 4 3 2 1   17 18 19 20 21 / 1

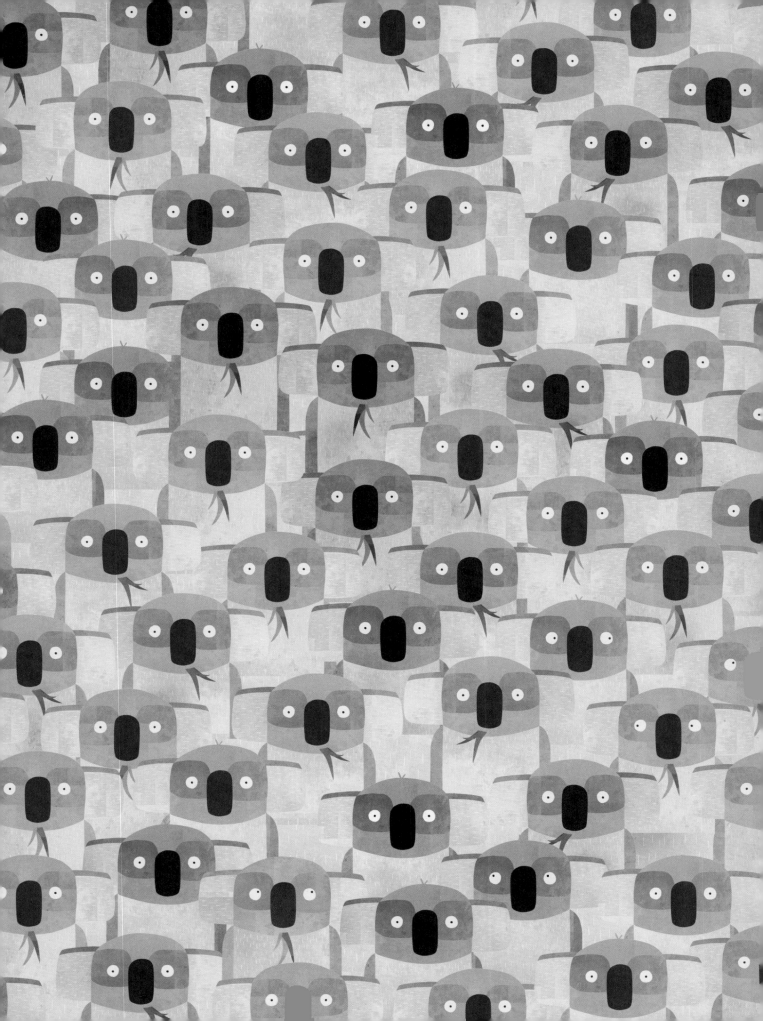

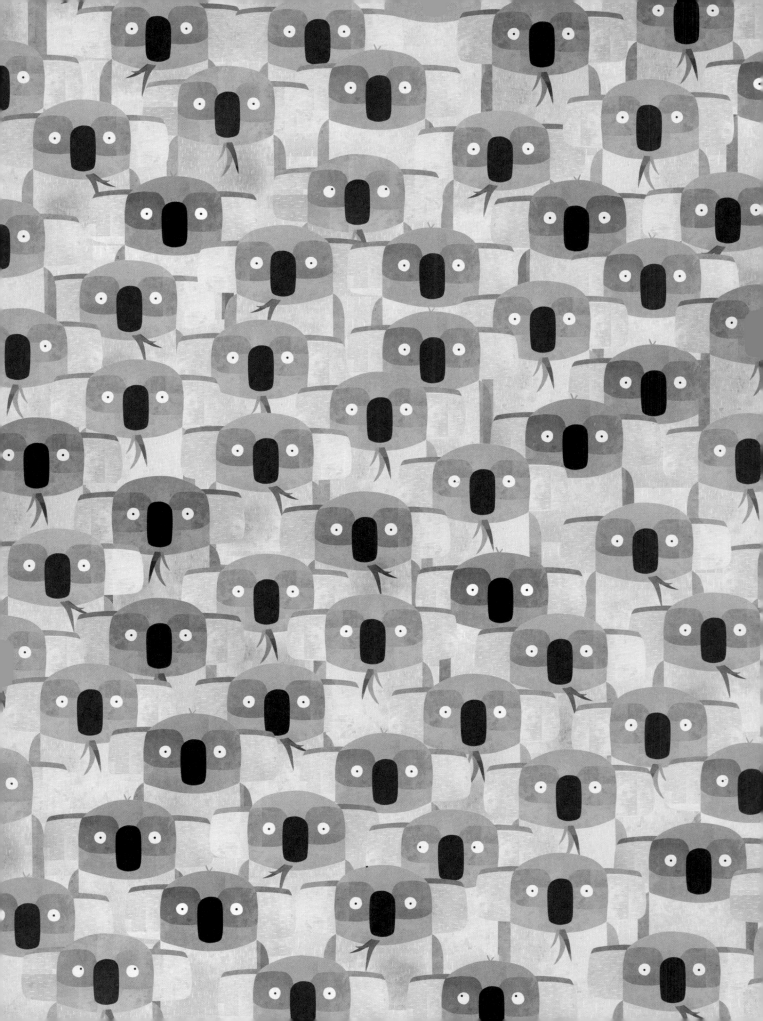